Granny Grimm's Gruesome Glasses

Jenny Nimmo and David Wynn Millward

Collins

Look out for more *Jets* from Collins

First published by A & C Black Ltd in 1995
Published by Collins in 1995
10 9 8 7 6 5 4
Collins is an imprint of HarperCollins*Publishers*Ltd,
77–85 Fulham Palace Road, Hammersmith, London W6 8JB

ISBN 0 00 675107 5

Text © Jenny Nimmo 1995
Illustrations © David Wynn Millward 1995

The author and the illustrator assert the moral right to
be identified as the author and the illustrator of the work.
A CIP record for this title is available from the British Library.

Printed and bound in Great Britain by
Omnia Books Ltd, Glasgow

Chapter 1

Fiona Smiley lived in a ramshackle house with broken gutters and dirty windows.

The paint was peeling and the gate wouldn't close properly.

No one in Fiona's family had time to mend things. They were always too busy being brainy.

Her father was a Professor of
Ancient History.

Her mother spoke nine languages
and often advised the government
on foreign affairs.

Her brother, Brian, was a computer wizard. Fiona thought he was even beginning to look like a computer.

Fiona hated not being brainy. She wondered if braininess had something to do with wearing glasses. Her mother, her father and her brother all wore glasses but none of them would let her borrow theirs.

So, one night, when they were asleep, Fiona tiptoed around the house trying on all their glasses.

But it was no use.
Brian's made things look too big.

Professor Smiley's glasses turned
things upside-down . . .

. . . and Mrs Smiley's carried things
so far away, Fiona couldn't see
them at all.

So next morning, Fiona went to the chemist's on her way to school to buy herself a pair of glasses.

She chose a pair of glasses with huge blue frames and rose-tinted lenses. Fiona thought they made her look really brainy.

But her friend, Tracy, said she looked 'naff'.

Arguing always gave Fiona a headache, and the glasses didn't help one bit when she tried to do her fractions.

Fiona stomped home feeling really miserable. But just as she was trying to close her garden gate, something caught her eye – A PAIR OF GLASSES!

They were sitting on the wall right in front of her,

a pair of neat gold-rimmed glasses just her size!

Fiona was too excited to notice Granny Grimm, who owned the glasses, standing on the other side of the wall.

Hold the bus, Sophie. I've got something in my eye.

BUS STOP

Gold-rimmed glasses! Maybe they'll do the trick...

Without stopping to think, Fiona
snatched off her rose-tinted glasses
and put on the gold-rimmed pair.

That's better. Now where are my specs?

I'll just try them on.

When Fiona put on the glasses,
things didn't just look different.
They FELT different.

OOPS! I feel all girlish.

WOW! I feel wobbly.

Fiona tried to run towards her house, but her legs felt peculiar. And when she looked down to see what had happened, she found that the only Fiona-ish things about her were her feet.

Just then,
Brian came
outside, and
believing
Granny
Grimm
to be Fiona,
called her
in for tea.

Granny Grimm, who never refused
an invitation, ran after Brian, into
Fiona's house and into Fiona's life.
While Fiona stood by, too dizzy to
move.

Chapter 2

Fiona tried to shout at Brian, but her
voice made a croaky sound and no
words came out. She was about to
chase after him when a girl grabbed
hold of her arm and dragged her
towards a bus.

Get your skates on, Gran, or we'll miss the bus!

I don't want a bus. I live here.

The girl took no notice of Fiona's
feeble cries and Fiona was
too weak to escape.
Before she knew what was
happening, the girl
had shoved her
on to the
bus.

OOOF!

Fiona stood in the aisle feeling horribly breathless.

Have my seat, Granny Grimm. Give your legs a rest.

I don't want your seat, I'm a child.

Come on, Gran. Don't be difficult

Fiona tried to keep calm. She had been turned into someone else. Transbodified. Perhaps it had something to do with the glasses? She gave the glasses a tug. They wouldn't budge. They seemed to be glued to her skin. Fiona gave a loud moan.

THEY'RE STUCK!

At the next stop the girl, who seemed to be Fiona's minder, pulled Fiona to her feet and guided her firmly off the bus.

Fiona didn't have the strength to run away. She followed the girl into a strange house and sat down at a long table in a very tidy kitchen. Besides the girl, whose name was Sophie, there were three other people in the kitchen. A boy of about eight, an almost middle-aged man, and a small blonde woman.

All the Grimms were very neat and tidy and didn't smile much. None of them wore glasses. When Fiona tried to tell them that she was not Granny Grimm, they didn't believe her.

Mrs Grimm just put a plate of horrible-looking food in front of her.

Chapter 3

After tea Fiona was helped into the sitting room and plonked in front of the television.

Fiona didn't like to argue with Mrs Grimm, so she took the cardigan and began to knit.

It took Fiona less than an hour to finish the cardigan. She seemed to have inherited Granny Grimm's gift for speed-knitting.

Mrs Grimm and Sophie helped Fiona upstairs to her room.

Suddenly Sophie noticed Fiona's trainers.

Mrs Grimm and Sophie left the room looking very cross, and Fiona was left alone.

She tugged at the glasses.

When Fiona saw the intercom she
had a brilliant idea. She waited
until the whole house was asleep,
and then shouted the rudest words
she could think of. Words that most
grannies probably hadn't even
heard of.

Exhausted by her dreadful evening
Fiona lay back and drifted off to
sleep, wondering if
the real Granny
Grimm was enjoying
being Fiona.

Chapter 4

When Fiona woke up she thought that she was back in her own room with the peeling wallpaper and the friendly mouse. But it was only an illusion. She could hear Sophie and Sam getting ready for school and longed to be with them.

She got out of bed as fast as she could, and put on her clothes.

When she
was dressed,
Fiona crept
downstairs
without
making
a sound.

Where do you think you're going?

Fiona wrenched open the door and made a dash for the gate. She tried leapfrogging, a talent for which she'd been famous, but her legs weren't as supple as they used to be.

Serves you right! Now go upstairs and change your muddy clothes.

AWWWW

Fiona trudged
up to her room
without stopping
to have her
breakfast. She
had never realized
how stiff old people's
legs could become.

At eleven o'clock
Mrs Grimm brought her
a cup of tea and a biscuit.

For lunch Fiona was given hard
peas and something that looked like
boot leather.

After their meal Mrs Grimm took
Fiona shopping. This involved a
great deal of queuing, and Fiona
wished she could have brought a
walking stick.

Just as they were leaving Savepounds Supermarket, Fiona saw an amazing sight. There, bold as brass, was Brian, HOLDING HANDS WITH A GIRL! Fiona leapt towards him. After a struggle, Brian managed to tear himself away and Fiona was led home in disgrace.

That evening she lay in her gloomy room, listening to the Grimms grumbling voices in the room below.

Sam brought Fiona a cup of cocoa before he went to bed. He didn't seem as grim as the rest of the family so Fiona decided to ask for his help.

Fiona drew a picture of herself as she used to be, so that Sam would recognize her.

Chapter 5

The next day, Fiona didn't attempt to leave the house. She waited eagerly for Sam's report. Mrs Grimm made her watch television, but when she had gone, Fiona switched it off.

She looked for something else to do.
In a corner of the room she found a
pile of D.I.Y. magazines. Fiona
settled down to read. It was
fascinating. She discovered all the
things she'd longed to know.

Fiona was so absorbed in the magazines she didn't hear Sophie and Sam come home from school. And when they had tea, she didn't hear a word anyone said. She was thinking of all the things she could do in her old home, if she ever got back there.

After tea, Sam came up to Fiona's room. 'I've seen a girl just like the one in your picture,' he told Fiona. 'She was in the park.'

'I ran up to her and told her she was my gran,' Sam said, 'but she didn't agree. And her friend told me to leave her alone or she'd go to the police.'

The next day Mrs Grimm took
Fiona to the post office to fetch her
pension.

While Mrs Grimm was queuing for
fish, Fiona slipped into the D.I.Y.
shop next door.

The man behind the counter looked rather surprised when he saw Fiona's list.

One large hammer

Three dozen medium-sized nails

Tube of wood glue

3 spanners in different sizes

BULLGRIP

STICK WOOD GLUE

2 sizes of tap washer

Fuses

Mrs Grimm was very suspicious of Fiona's bulging D.I.Y. bag.

When she got home, Fiona rushed upstairs and hid the bag under the bed.

Chapter 6

On Saturday morning, Sam kept his
word and took Fiona to Savepounds
Supermarket. And there, standing
by the entrance, was Fiona, or
rather Granny Grimm looking like
Fiona.

Granny Grimm was now very
nimble, even in her granny shoes.
She nipped into the supermarket
and vanished into a sea of trolleys.

Fiona began to feel breathless, her old bones were playing up.

Granny Grimm slipped out of
Fiona's grasp, leaving her holding
nothing but a red ribbon.

Fiona was so exhausted after the long chase, Sam agreed to wheel her home in the trolley.

Fiona had never felt so disheartened in her whole life. But there was worse to come.

When they got home, Mrs Grimm
was looking grimmer than ever.

Fiona almost fainted when she saw
the list of things she had to pack.

LIST
2 prs long pants
2 prs thick vests
2 cardis
Woollen hat
2 prs wool tights
1 nice dress
2 thick nighties
Duffle coat
2 petticoats
1 thick scarf
Walking boots
Hot water bottle
AND DON'T FORGET YOUR KNITTING!

Fiona spent the weekend in a daze.
With a heavy heart she washed and
ironed the clothes she'd been told
to pack.

On Sunday afternoon, Fiona felt so gloomy she flopped down in a big armchair and turned on the television. The doorbell rang but she took no notice. And then Sam appeared.

It's for you.

Who is it?

It's a surprise.

I hope it's a nice one.

Sam winked at Fiona as she passed him. Fiona was mystified – who would want to visit her? As she reached the open front door, she couldn't believe her eyes, for there, on the step was the real Granny Grimm.

Sam suggested that Fiona and
Granny Grimm swop glasses at
exactly the same moment.

Off came Granny Grimm's
gruesome glasses.
Off came the rose-tinted glasses.

Just for a moment Sam was confused. Then he saw the shoes and he knew who was who.

He ran to get Fiona's D.I.Y. bag and when Granny Grimm heard where her pension money had gone, she gave Fiona her wholehearted approval.

You need it, dear.

Before she left, Fiona asked Sam to make a promise.

And then Granny Grimm took Fiona back to her ramshackle house.

When Fiona entered the house, she was surprised to find Brian cowering behind a chair in the sitting room.

When Fiona had dealt with Brian
she started fixing the house.

First she changed
the tap washer.

Then she mended
the fuse.

She cleaned
the gutter.

She fixed the
broken chair.

She patched
the cracks
in the wall.

And then
she set to
work in the
garden.

Of course, Professor and Mrs
Smiley were far too busy to notice
Fiona doing all these things.
But Brian was most impressed.

In no time at all the ramshackle
house was really comfortable. Fiona
became quite famous for doing-it-
herself. She could mend anything,
anywhere, and before long she had
earned enough money to buy
herself a workbench, a power drill
and a tool-box with spanners and
screwdrivers in seven different sizes.

63

A month later, Fiona invited Sam and Granny Grimm to tea, and they all agreed that life was pretty good.